The Witch Next Door
and Other Stories

Stories and pictures by
NORMAN BRIDWELL

SCHOLASTIC INC.

New York   Toronto   London   Auckland   Sydney
Mexico City   New Delhi   Hong Kong   Buenos Aires

The Witch Next Door, ISBN 0-590-40433-4, Copyright © 1986, 1965 by Norman Bridwell.

The Witch Grows Up, ISBN 0-590-40559-4, Copyright © 1979 by Norman Bridwell.

The Witch Goes to School, ISBN 0-590-45831-0, Copyright © 1992 by Norman Bridwell.

The Witch's Vacation, ISBN 0-590-40558-6, Copyright © 1973 by Norman Bridwell.

12 11 10 9 8 7 6 5 4 3 2 1   4 5 6 7 8 9/0

Printed in the U.S.A.   24
This edition created exclusively for Barnes & Noble, Inc.
2004 Barnes & Noble Books
ISBN 0-7607-5802-6
First compilation printing, September 2004

The Witch Next Door

The Witch
Next Door

To Timothy Howard

There is a witch living on our street.
Do you know how I can tell?

It's nothing you would notice
the first time you saw her.

It isn't the way she says hello.

Maybe it's the way she does her shopping.
You might know then.

I thought she was a witch the very day she moved in.

And I was sure of it when she painted her house.
Black isn't my favorite color,
but after all, it's her house.

You might notice her washing on Monday mornings.

Or you might be surprised
when she takes her pets for a walk.

She's a good neighbor.
She keeps her house very neat.

If someone is sick, she sends him
cookies and hot soup.

When you have a kite up a tree,
she is always ready to lend a hand.

And if you don't have a kite,
she takes care of that, too.

She's a wonderful neighbor.
Oh, she does cast a few spells now and then.

But they don't hurt anybody.

And she's very quiet.
She goes to sleep at eight o'clock every night . . .

. . .except once in a while
when her friends come to a cook-out.

She's very good to us.
She showed us the bat bath in her yard.

We had so much fun with our witch.
And then . . .

. . . one day we were at her house
having tea and cookies.
There was a knock at the door.

It was the people next door.
They didn't look very happy.

"You had better move," they said.
"We don't want witches in our neighborhood."

Well! Our witch got angry.
I'd never seen her like that before.

We were angry, too.

So our witch cast a spell on them.

It was terrible. I couldn't look.

She changed them into a handsome young prince and princess.

Of course they forgot about
asking our witch to leave.

I asked the witch to change *us* into a
beautiful prince and princess.

But she said no.
She said good boys and girls
are more beautiful than
princes and princesses.

The Witch Grows Up

The Witch Grows Up

For Joshua

The lady who lives next door is a witch.
She is our friend.

One day we asked her, "What was it like when you were a little girl?"

She said her mother and father were witches. They were glad when they knew they were going to have a baby.

They made a special cradle for the new baby.

She had toys, dolls, and stuffed animals.

When her daddy came home, he would
toss her into the air . . . .

When she didn't want to eat, her mother had ways of getting her to eat.

She had a wading pool . . .

and a jungle gym.

Sometimes she would talk back to her mother and father.

She learned not to do that.

When she was a little older, she played
with other kids. She had her own jump rope.

She was good at tag.

Very good!

When the boys wouldn't let her
use their tree house . . .

she didn't care. The tree
was a friend of hers.

Her mother was like a lot of mothers. She wanted her little girl to take music lessons.

She listened to the little witch play her violin every day.

When the little witch was old enough,
she went to school.

She went to witch school.

All the little witches took cooking
lessons. They didn't make cupcakes.

They cooked up other things.

They studied spelling.

She learned some good spells.

And she learned to ride on a broom.

She was good at that.

When school was out she rushed home,
because that was the best place in the world.

Every night at bedtime her father
read her a story.

And her bed tucked her in.

The little witch had good dreams.

You see, little witches
are just like you and me.

The Witch
Goes to School

To Mary Gentle
—N.B.

The Witch
Goes to School

Our next-door neighbor is a good friend of ours. She also happens to be a witch.

One day we were late for school. Our witch said she would get us there on time.

And she did.

We got to our room just before
the bell rang. Our teacher was surprised.

She invited the witch to stay for a visit.
It was show-and-tell time. Kevin showed us
his tooth that came out that morning.

I said I had lost one of my teeth, but I forgot to bring it to school. The witch just waved her hands. . . .

The tooth fairy
flew in. She had
my tooth.

She said I could have a quarter if I let
her keep it, so I did. She gave Kevin
a quarter for his tooth, too.

The tooth fairy was the hit of show-and-tell time. After she left, we did silent reading. That is always fun.

I was sure that I saw real dinosaurs come out of my brother's book. I thought our witch was working her magic.

She said she wasn't. Books are like that.
Sometimes they seem real.

At recess, we all ran outside.
I wanted to get to the slide first.
The slide is my favorite.

The witch made the slide more
fun than it had ever been before.

And she turned the jungle gym into a real jungle.

Then there was some trouble.
A big kid wouldn't let a little kid
come down from the seesaw.

Our witch doesn't like that kind of teasing.

After recess, we had writing.
I couldn't think of anything
good to write about.

I asked the witch to
help me. She wouldn't.
She said that wouldn't
be fair.

I tried a little harder and I wrote a story
I was really proud of.

It was about the day our witch came
to school!

We went to the cafeteria for lunch.

That big kid was there. He grabbed my brother's peanut butter sandwich.

Then the sandwich grabbed him. What a mess!

One of the cafeteria
ladies gets upset if we
don't eat all our food.

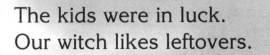

The kids were in luck.
Our witch likes leftovers.

She felt a little full....

But she was fine by the time we walked back
to our classroom.

That afternoon, we went on a nature walk.
Our teacher said that we would see some
interesting animals.

She was right. We saw mice, birds, rabbits, and squirrels.

We even found a frog and a snail.

Then the witch showed us some animals that we had never seen in the woods before.

What an exciting field trip!
The animals took us for rides.

Then we said good-bye
and walked back to school.

Our teacher thanked our witch for making the day so much fun. Our witch thanked our teacher for making every day so special.

The Witch's Vacation

The Witch's Vacation

For Joseph

We know a witch! She lives next door.
My brother and I have so much fun with
her, we never like to go away from home.

But last summer we had to go to camp. We felt
bad because the witch wasn't coming with us.

It was raining when we got to camp. They
gave us a tent number. But when we saw
the tent, we were afraid to go inside.

What a surprise!

We put on our bathing suits and went up on the porch with the other campers. We wished it would stop raining. Then I saw something funny. In one spot on the beach it was not raining at all. And guess who was there waving at us?

We were so glad that our witch was with us again.
The other kids thought she was funny-looking.
One of them made fun of her bathing suit.

The witch just smiled and turned him into a terrific swimmer.

But just for a minute. Then she gave all the
kids some water wings to play with.

My brother built a sand castle, but a big
kid knocked it down. It didn't matter. . . .

The witch helped my brother build another
sand castle.

The next day she packed a picnic basket. We
ate on her picnic tablecloth.

Then everyone hiked to Lookout Point. The big kids left us far behind. The witch just smiled. She said WE would get to the top first.

One night the cook couldn't get the campfire going. It looked as if we would not have a weenie roast that night.

Our good old witch came to the rescue.

Having a witch at camp makes a big difference.
It was turning out to be a wonderful vacation.

Our witch was there the day I wanted to go
riding. There was just one horse left. The
kids called her "Old Nellie-Bones."

I called her "Nellie the Great."

And she was.

One day I took out a rowboat so my brother could go fishing. He wasn't having much luck until . . .

the witch let him use her broom
for a fishing pole.

After a while, the witch went ashore
to take a nap.

We were having so much fun that we didn't see where we were going.

There was a waterfall ahead and we couldn't stop.

We tried the witch's broom. It only works
for witches.

I wished for the witch as hard as I could.

Back at the camp the witch woke up. She
knew we were in trouble.

But she didn't have her broom. How could
she get to us in time?

In a wink, she changed the water to ice—

and rushed to save us. Good old witch.

We flew back to camp.

The witch changed the ice back to water, and we celebrated by having a swimming party.

It was the best vacation ever, thanks to our witch.